ght you might
sexy story -
explain it

- Love
Herman
X

A CAT AND MOUSE LOVE STORY

NANETTE NEWMAN

PICTURES BY
MICHAEL FOREMAN

Heinemann·Quixote

For
Bryan, Sarah and Emma

— *N.N.*

Louise, Mark and Ben

— *M.F.*

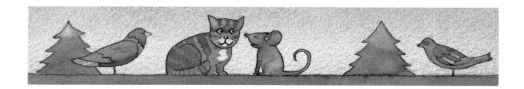

Heinemann/Quixote Press
10 Upper Grosvenor Street, London W1X 9PA
LONDON   MELBOURNE   TORONTO
JOHANNESBURG   AUCKLAND

Copyright © text Bryan Forbes Ltd., 1984
Copyright © illustrations Michael Foreman 1984
First published 1984

SBN: 434 98045 5

Origination by Imago Publishing Limited
Printed in Hong Kong

A CAT AND MOUSE LOVE STORY

The saga I'll tell, in the form of a story,
Is of love and despair, and of joy and of glory,
You mustn't just snigger and say "fancy that"
When I say it's about a young mouse and a cat.

Leola, the cat, was in no way just catty,
She was fiery and wiry, and sometimes quite ratty.
Jasper, the mouse (a hero to come),
Was poetic and charming, and sometimes quite dumb!

I'll start with their meeting (I don't know just why)
Except it's so touching you may want to cry.

THE MEETING

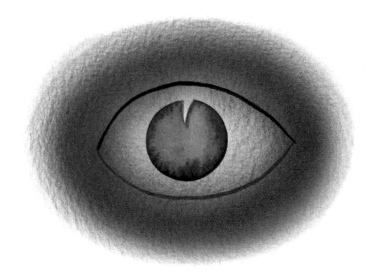

Having peacefully lived in a hole, in a clock,
Jasper one morning awoke with a shock!

He looked out of the darkness, and there did behold,
A large yellow cat's eye, which instantly rolled.
It stared straight at poor Jasper as if to say
"Get down on your knees, you've approached your last day."

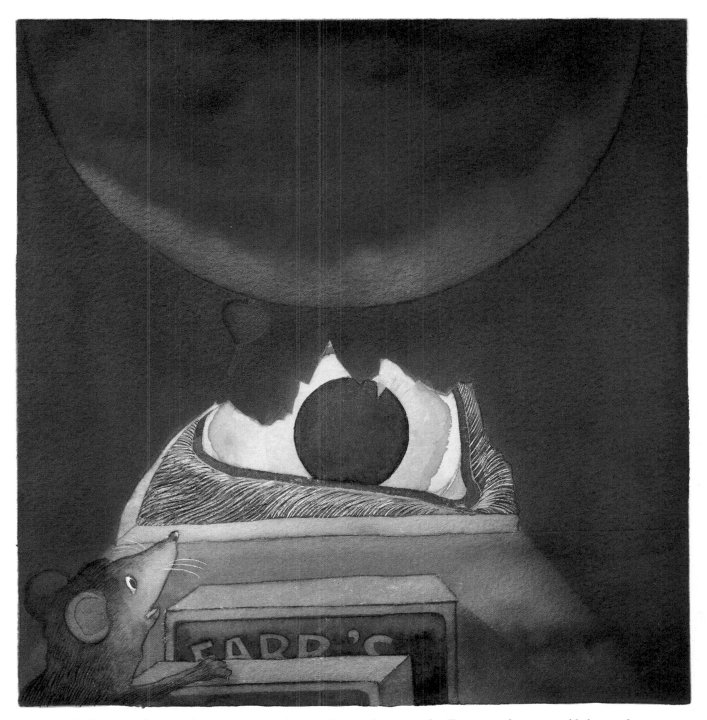

Many thoughts started racing through Jasper's small head,
The most fervent of which was that soon he'd be dead.
He growled and he spat, and he barked like a dog,
And he shouted rude things like "Get out beastly mog!"

The eye didn't blink, didn't waver or go,
But stared at his antics – like watching a show.

Eventually worn out with growling and spitting,
Poor Jasper decided 'twas time for some hitting.
He punched at the eye, with a tightly curled fist,
But the eye simply blinked, so he had to desist.

It was while he was hitting, his brain seemed to say:
"That eye is so lovely, I wish it could stay."

He stopped and he stared, his heart started to pound,
For he knew in a flash , it was love he had found.
He immediately sat and wrote in big writing,
"I LOVE YOU, MY DARLING –
          PLEASE, LET'S STOP THIS FIGHTING."

THE DAWNING OF LOVE

For a second the eye began clouding with doubt,
Then a tear bubbled up and came tumbling out.
"Love" thought Leola (though a mother of eight)
Was a feeling that she had left much, *much* too late!

She was scraggy and mangy, and fought for her life,
And no-one had *ever* said "Please be my wife."

So instead of just killing this strange little mouse,
She went stumbling and fainting all over the house.
But Jasper soon found her and said, "It's no trick,"
"I love you, Leola – please marry me quick."

In his eyes she was beautiful, sleek and divine,
So he fell on one knee and said, "Please, *please* be mine."

They were married that day, to the horror of many,
By the dog round the corner called Reverend Benny.

"Will you take this old cat?" – Jasper said, "Oh yes, rather"
(Eight small kittens all sighed, they'd at last got a father).

DISASTER STRIKES

I wish I could state life was smooth ever after,
But they soon were to have their first major disaster.
Before even the honeymoon came to an end
A cloud on their life had begun to descend.

How *could* Jasper have known, he never foresaw,
That on Thursday – at noon – he'd be called up "to war".
A letter arrived to this innocent pair, saying
"Jasper – war started – you'd better be there."
He stared at the paper, and stuttered "Great rats",
For the mice were at war with – you've guessed it – the cats.

Leola just cried at this terrible blow,
"The cats will all kill you – I can't let you go."

Said Jasper, "The mice have been planning this folly –
If I *had* to fight, I might kill your Aunt Dolly!"
They both sat in silence, for no words were needed,
With no hate in their hearts now that love had succeeded.

Quite suddenly Jasper leapt up in the air,
"I've thought of a plan, if we only could dare."
His plan was so simple, direct and quite plain,
To convince cats and mice that they'd nothing to gain
By constantly hating and killing and fighting –
That to love one another was *much* more exciting.

THE PLAN

They started that night, for they'd no time to waste,
They knew this was something that had to be faced!

At a house the next day mice were ready and lurking,
Over the wall, cats were stalking and smirking.

The Mouse Sergeant was giving instructions in fighting,
Shouting "Punch, spit, kick, push and don't forget biting."

A tom cat with one ear, who was known as "Hot Shot",
Could be heard calmly hissing, "I'll swallow the lot!"

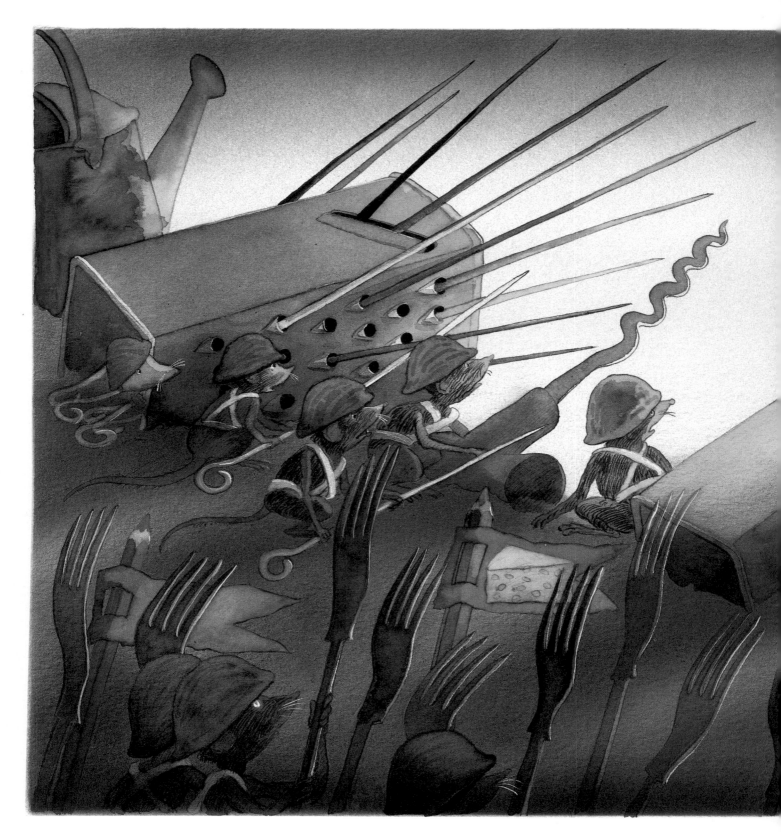

It was at this tense moment that Jasper leapt out,
His courage, thought Leola, no-one could doubt.

He said, "I would like all you animals to know
I have love in my heart – and I want it to show."

He rushed up to a cat who was staring aghast
And gave him a badge which said "TRUE FRIENDS AT LAST".

Leola, on cue, did the same to a mouse
And hearts missed a beat all around that dark house.

The Sergeant just stared as if he was dreaming,
"Hot Shot" was so stunned, he forgot all his scheming.
Leola then asked the mouse "Mean Melanie"
If tomorrow she'd care to come over for tea.

Then Jasper to Henry (the cruellest of all)
Said, "Eat cheese with me one night outside my back wall."

Then gradually – seeing the sense of all this –
The Sergeant gave Tabatha's left paw a kiss!
Some smiles then broke out, 'stead of hissing and snarling,
The scene as one watched was amazing and charming!
Then onto a box Jasper climbed midst applause
and said:
"Friends, cats and mice people,
Pull in your claws.

No more fighting and killing,
It's wasteful and sad –
All this loathing each other
Just has to be bad.
If we learn how to love
One and all, and each other,
We will then proudly say –
This cat here is my brother.''

So everyone cheered, and some gently cried,
They said,
"Isn't it wondrous?
No cat or mouse died!
It's nicer to love, if you give it a chance,
The warring has ended, so let's sing and dance."

Leola the cat and Jasper the mouse
Went home happy that night to their own little house.
Some people might say that their victory was small,
But the truth of the matter is *love* conquers all.

The End
(a happy one thanks to Jasper)